The author and publisher are indebted to Diane Melvin, child psychologist, for her invaluable help in the preparation of this book.

First published in 1989 by Conran Octopus Limited
This edition first published in Britain in 2002 by Brimax,
an imprint of Octopus Publishing Group Ltd
2-4 Heron Quays, London E14 4JP

McGraw-Hill Children's Publishing

This edition published in the United States in 2002 by
McGraw-Hill Children's Publishing,
a Division of The McGraw-Hill Companies
8787 Orion Place
Columbus, OH 43240

www.MHkids.com

Printed in China.

1-57768-988-7

Library of Congress Cataloging-in-Publication Data is on file with the publisher.

1 2 3 4 5 6 7 8 9 BRI 07 06 07 05 04 03 02

The McGraw-Hill Companies

First Experiences

Lucy's New House

Written by **Barbara Taylor Cork**

Illustrated by **Siobhan Dodds**

McGraw-Hill Children's Publishing

Columbus, Ohio

This is Lucy and her brother, Ryan. Soon they will be moving to a new house.

Today, the family that bought Lucy and Ryan's house has come to look at it. Mom shows the family around.

After they leave, Lucy feels sad and angry.

"I don't want anyone else sleeping in my room," she says.

"Cheer up," says Mom. "In our new house, you'll have a room of your very own."

"Let's go see the new house," Dad says.
On the way, they pass a big park. The playground is full of children.

At the new house, Ryan and Lucy see their new bedrooms.

"Your bed will fit in this corner," Mom says to Lucy, "and there's lots of room for your toys in here."

Today is Lucy's last morning at her school.
She will go to a new school near her new house.
The children and the teacher give her a present.

Lucy and her friend, Sally, are sad to say goodbye. "Sally can come and visit us in our new house very soon," says Mom.

When Lucy and Mom get home, Ryan and Dad are busy packing things into big boxes.

Lucy helps Mom sort out her old clothes.

On moving day, Ryan and Lucy wake up early.
The movers arrive with a big truck.

The movers help the family pack up everything into boxes.

The movers carry the heavy furniture and boxes to the truck. When they have finished, the house doesn't look like Ryan and Lucy's home anymore.

Mom puts Fluff, the cat, into her carrier, and then puts her in the car.

"Off we go," says Dad, cheerfully. The children wave goodbye to their old house.

At the new house, Lucy and Ryan are very excited. Their footsteps sound very loud when they run around the empty rooms.

"Come and have lunch before the moving truck gets here," says Mom, unpacking the picnic she has made. They sit on the floor to eat.

Soon the movers arrive. Mom tells them where to put everything.

When some of the boxes are unpacked, the house begins to look like home.

Mom and Dad are very tired. Moving is hard work.

Ryan and Lucy go outside to play. Their yard is much larger than their old one.

Lucy likes her new house and her new yard, but she misses her old friends.

"Time for bed," Mom says. "Ryan, you can sleep in Lucy's room tonight." Lucy is happy that she does not have to sleep by herself.

Lucy is happy to be in her own bed, with her toys. The bedroom feels almost like their old room. "We'll unpack the rest of your things in the morning," says Mom, kissing them goodnight.

The next morning, the doorbell rings.

"Is this your cat?" asks a little girl. "I found her in my yard. I'm Amy. I live next door."

"Yes, thank you. Her name is Fluff, and mine is Lucy," she replies.

Lucy invites Amy to see her new room.

"What a cool room," says Amy. "I'm glad you've come to live next door!"

"So am I!" says Lucy, smiling at her new friend. "I'm glad I moved."